THE BIRTHDAY VISITOR

Yoshiko Uchida

THE BIRTHDAY VISITOR

Illustrated by Charles Robinson

CHARLES SCRIBNER'S SONS
NEW YORK

For H.

Also by Yoshiko Uchida

SAMURAI OF GOLD HILL

JOURNEY TO TOPAZ

HISAKO'S MYSTERIES

SUMI & THE GOAT & THE TOKYO EXPRESS

SUMI'S SPECIAL HAPPENING

SUMI'S PRIZE

THE FOREVER CHRISTMAS TREE

When Emi Watanabe walked home from school, she usually walked slowly and kept her eyes on the ground, for there were so many interesting things to be found. Once she had found a silver button and, another time, a bright red feather and an agate marble. Just the other day, she'd found a shiny penny with an Indian's head on it instead of Mr. Lincoln's, and Papa told her to put it away carefully and not spend it on candy.

Sometimes she watched so she wouldn't step on a single crack in the sidewalk all the way home. Benji Tamura, who lived next door, had told her, "Step on a crack, break your mother's back." And Emi certainly didn't want to be responsible for breaking Mama's back.

Today, however, Emi was in a hurry and she didn't have time to keep her eyes on the ground even though she might miss something interesting. For today was Friday, and on Fridays she always stopped to see Mr. and Mrs. Wada on her way home from school.

Mama told her they were old and lonely and looked forward to her visit each week. Furthermore, Emi liked going there. Mrs. Wada always had something nice for her, like a fresh batch of butter cookies, or a sponge cake, or a cup of steaming cocoa. And Mr. Wada would stir up the water in his pond so she could see his big speckled carp.

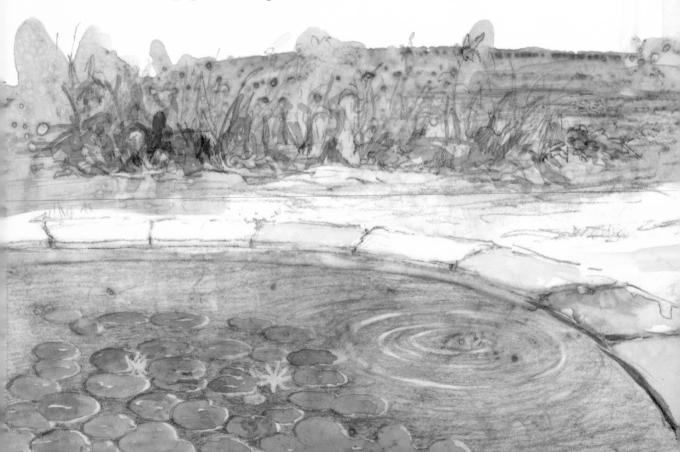

Today Emi was anxious to tell Mrs. Wada about the man from Japan who was coming to spoil her birthday next week. Mrs. Wada would cluck sympathetically and perhaps make her feel better about the whole thing. She certainly didn't feel good about it now.

Emi swung open the squeaky gate to their backyard and found old Mr. Wada sitting in a canvas chair, wearing his eyeshade and taking a little nap. His wrinkled face looked half green beneath the celluloid shade.

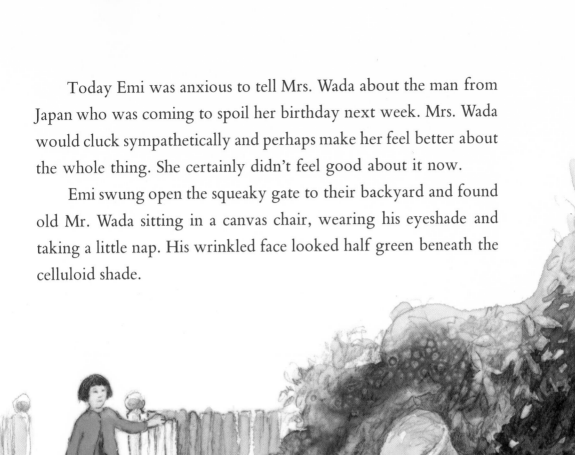

"Hello, Ojii-chan," Emi called in a loud voice. He liked being called Grandpa, since he didn't have any grandchildren of his own.

Mr. Wada bestirred himself and smiled at Emi. "Ah, come to see us at last, have you?" he shouted, as though she were just as deaf as he.

Emi went to his good ear and shouted back, "I was here last Friday."

But Mr. Wada didn't pay attention to what she said. "Well now, would you like to see my old friend in the pond?" he asked cheerfully. And without waiting for an answer, he got up creakily and stirred the murky water of his fish pond. In a moment, the enormous speckled carp nosed his way to the surface, nipping the old man's finger as though it were a delicious worm.

"Hello there, old friend," Mr. Wada greeted him warmly. "How do you feel today? Look who's come to see us."

"Wouldn't you rather have a pet dog, Ojii-chan?" Emi asked as she watched. A dog would at least wag his tail and lick his hand, she thought.

But the old man shook his head. "What could be nicer than a pet carp?" he asked. "He doesn't bark, he doesn't dig up the moss in my garden, and he doesn't have to be walked. He just lives peacefully at the bottom of his pond and lets me be. When I want to see him, I just stir up the water and there he is."

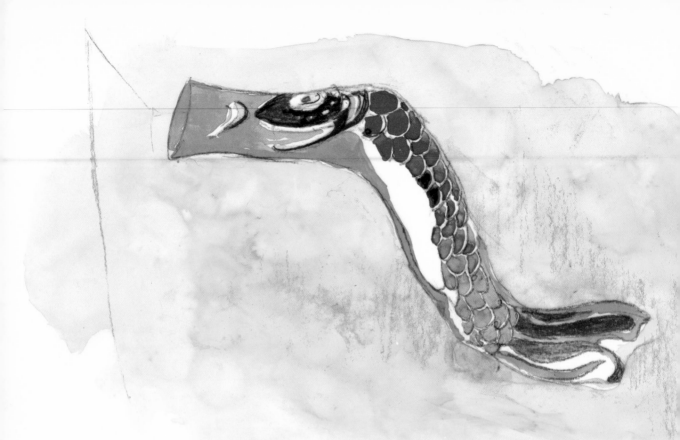

Emi had to agree there was something to that, but as for her, she wouldn't trade her dog, Wanko, for all the carp in the world. The only carp in their house was a big cloth one which swam on a pole in the river of the sky for Boys' Day. Since she wasn't a boy, they flew their carp for Papa, and on Dolls Festival Day Mama put out her Japanese doll collection for Emi.

Emi left Mr. Wada talking to his carp and ran inside to see Mrs. Wada.

"Obaa-chan," she called. Then she sniffed happily. Something smelled wonderfully good.

"*Mah*, Emi-chan, I'm so glad you've come," Mrs. Wada said, as though she hadn't seen her for ten years. "You're just in time for a piece of sponge cake."

She cut a thick slice for Emi and put it on the kitchen table with a glass of milk. Emi sat down, took a big mouthful of cake, and didn't even wait for Mrs. Wada to ask about school or Mama and Papa.

"A horrid man is coming to spoil my birthday," she said dismally. "He's a minister coming from Japan. And he's going to stay all week!"

Emi didn't like visiting ministers from Japan. They were mostly very proper and very dull and absolutely no fun at all. Both Mama and Papa had come from Japan to live in California and now their friends at the Christian University in Kyoto sent all kinds of friends, and even friends of friends, to visit them when they came to America. Sometimes they spent the night with them. Sometimes they spent two nights. Now this minister, the Reverend Kichisaburo Okura, was going to stay a whole week. Not only that, he was arriving right on her birthday.

"*Mah,*" Mrs. Wada said. "Do you mean to say he is arriving on the very day of your seventh birthday? On Tuesday? On November 14?"

Emi nodded three times to answer each of her questions. "So I can't have a party."

"Ah, that is too bad," Mrs. Wada said, and she clucked sympathetically, just as Emi knew she would.

"He's going to spoil my whole, entire birthday," Emi said darkly.

Mrs. Wada tipped her head and thought for a moment. "Maybe he won't," she said softly. "Maybe he will be very nice. He just might surprise you."

But Emi knew he wouldn't, and she left Mrs. Wada's house not feeling any better than when she arrived, even though she was filled now with Obaa-chan's delicious sponge cake.

"Step, step, step, step. . . . Step on a crack. Break Rev. Okura's back," Emi said, and she put one foot down squarely on a crack.

But the moment she did, she was ashamed of herself. "I didn't really mean it," she said out loud to whoever was in charge of this game, and she ran the rest of the way home.

Benji was sitting on his front steps waiting for her. Benji was five and the other boys on the block wouldn't play with him because he was too young. That was why he played with Emi, even though she was a girl.

"Wanna play marbles?" he asked now.

Emi shook her head. She wanted to go ask Mama if Rev. Okura was really coming on Tuesday. Maybe he had changed his mind. Maybe he would come next year. Maybe he wouldn't come at all.

"Hello, Wanko," Emi called to her German shepherd. "Wait for me. I'll be out later."

Wanko wagged his tail and sat down to wait for her.

"Mama," Emi called as she walked into the house. "Is he still coming?"

Mama was ironing a big white tablecloth, which meant she was getting ready for company.

"Hello, Emi-chan," she said, and because she knew exactly who Emi was talking about, she answered, "Why, of course Rev. Okura is coming. His ship is in the middle of the ocean right now. It docks on Tuesday."

"My birthday," Emi said, as though Mama didn't know.

"We'll have a big cake and ice cream for dessert," Mama said.

But that wouldn't be like having her own special party with her friends as she usually did. Emi went back outside feeling sorry for herself.

"Benji!" she shouted over the fence. "I'll play marbles with you now." But Benji had disappeared, and only Wanko was there, still waiting.

Emi sat down on the back steps and felt like a black rain cloud. "Phooey!" she said.

Wanko wagged his tail and licked her hand.

Tuesday, November 14, was a beautiful day, and the sun made Emi's room as bright as a field of buttercups.

"Happy birthday, Emi-chan!" It was Mama with a new pink wool dress that she had made for Emi. She spread it out on her bed and she also gave Emi a big hug.

At breakfast Papa put down his newspaper and gave Emi another hug. "Happy birthday, Miss Seven-year-old," he said, and he watched, smiling, as she found the small box beside her plate. Inside was a gold heart-shaped locket on a thin gold chain. It was her present from Mama and Papa.

"Oh, Mama! Papa!" Emi was so excited, she couldn't put into words all the wonderful feelings that were jumping around inside of her.

"I've invited Mr. and Mrs. Wada to come for your birthday dinner too," Mama said. "We'll have a lovely celebration."

"Even with the minister?" Emi asked.

"Certainly," Mama answered.

"The ship docks at noon," Papa said. "I'll take the afternoon off from the office and we'll be home in plenty of time for supper."

Papa knew all about meeting ships at the pier in San Francisco, for he had met so many and brought home so many visitors from Japan.

Mama was already getting ready for dinner when Emi got home from school. The house smelled good. It smelled like the birthday cake Mama had baked in the morning. It smelled like the roast beef Mama had in the oven. And it smelled like the furniture polish that Mama used to dust the living room.

"Hello, birthday girl," Mama called. "Will you help me set the table?"

Emi helped Mama pull open the dining room table to put in an extra board. Together they spread the big white linen cloth over it, and Emi put out the silverware and the linen napkins and the glasses. Then she went outside to pick flowers for the centerpiece before Mama asked her to. She decided to pick a handful of the small red button chrysanthemums that were growing in Papa's flower garden.

"Is he here yet?" It was Benji, shouting to her over the fence. "Not yet," Emi hollered back. "Want to see my new dress?"

But Benji didn't care about new dresses. "I want to see the minister," he answered.

"He'll only be dull and boring," Emi shouted and ran into the house to put the chrysanthemums into the hollow back of Mama's cream-colored china swan.

Papa arrived home with Rev. Okura at exactly the same instant that Mr. and Mrs. Wada walked up the front steps. So there was a tremendous amount of bowing and talking and greeting on the front porch.

Mrs. Wada gave Emi a hug and admired her new pink dress and the gold locket. Mr. Wada was dressed in his best Sunday suit and had left his green eyeshade at home. They gave Emi her birthday present, which was a hand-carved music box from Switzerland.

"This is Rev. Okura," Papa said to Mama and Emi.

Mama bowed and told him how glad she was to meet him, but Emi thought for a minute that Papa had brought home the wrong man. Rev. Okura didn't look very dull or even very proper. He looked a little rumpled, as though he had just enjoyed a good game of baseball. He had thick, wavy black hair, a friendly grin, and shook Emi's hand so hard she felt her bones crunch. The first thing he said was, "I have a little girl just about your age."

The first thing Emi said was, "You don't look like a minister."

And that was when Benji came running over. "Look what I found," he shouted to everybody. Cupped in his hands was a small dead baby sparrow, its legs thrust stiffly into the air.

"Poor little bird," Mama said. "He must have fallen from his nest."

"Most likely," Papa and Mr. Wada agreed.

And Mrs. Wada clucked in sympathy over the small ball of fluff in Benji's hands.

"What'll I do with it?" Benji asked.

"Bury it beneath our peach tree and give it a funeral," Emi answered.

Then Rev. Okura spoke. "I'd be happy to help you with the funeral," he said, for he knew that was what his own little girl would have wanted.

And that was exactly what Emi wanted too. She had given her goldfish a funeral when she buried them, but of course, she didn't have a minister to help her then. Now here was a real live minister from Japan offering to give Benji's bird a funeral.

"Come to the backyard," she urged, and she led the way as everyone followed. Everyone, that is, except Mama who had to go inside and tend to her roast, and Papa who had to go to the drugstore to buy the ice cream for dessert.

Emi and Benji quickly dug a hole beneath the peach tree. Then they wrapped the bird in a leaf from the fig tree, put it in its grave, and heaped a mound of stones over it. Mrs. Wada picked one of Papa's chrysanthemums and placed it on top of the stones.

Then Rev. Okura clasped his hands together. "Dear God," he said, "we know you watch over even the smallest sparrow that falls. Bless this little creature we send into Your care."

"Love, Benji," Benji said, as though he were signing a letter.

Emi nudged him with her elbow. "Say Amen," she whispered. Benji didn't know anything, she thought, because he didn't go to Sunday School.

"Amen," Benji said.

Then Rev. Okura began to sing. He sang a Japanese hymn in a beautiful tenor voice, and when he got to the second verse, Mr. and Mrs. Wada joined in and sang with him.

It was the nicest funeral Emi had ever been to and she began to have a few warm feelings toward this Rev. Kichisaburo Okura from Japan.

Since Benji was there anyway, Mama told Emi to set a place at the table for him, and she telephoned his mama to tell her he would be staying for Emi's birthday dinner.

Benji thought that was a fine idea. He was also beginning to have good feelings about this minister who gave his bird such a nice funeral.

When dinner was over, Mr. Wada shouted in his loudest voice that he believed Mama's roast beef was the best he'd had since he came to America. And Mrs. Wada admired Mama's gravy which she said was as smooth as silk.

But Emi liked dessert best, for Mama had baked her a three-layer cake with chocolate frosting and decorated it with seven red candles and white icing letters that said, Happy Birthday Emi.

When she saw that cake and heard everyone sing "Happy Birthday" to her, she didn't care any more about not having had a special afternoon party. It was turning out to be a fine birthday after all.

When Mrs. Wada dropped her napkin, Emi crawled under the table to get it for her. That was when she saw two large black-stockinged feet wriggling in front of her nose. They didn't belong to Papa or to Mr. Wada, but to Rev. Okura himself.

Emi scrambled back to her chair and looked at Rev. Okura, wondering how he could sit there looking so proper, when under the table he had his shoes off and was wriggling his toes. Emi began to giggle and Rev. Okura seemed to know why. He grinned and then winked at her. Emi wanted to wink back, but she didn't know how. Instead, she reached in front of Benji and passed the bowl of salted almonds across the table.

"Here, Rev. Okura," she said grandly. "They're good."

After dinner, they all gathered around the piano. Mama played "Swanee River," and Papa and Mrs. Wada sang a duet just the way they did at church. Then Rev. Okura sang the books of the Bible to the tune of a Japanese folk song. It sounded so funny that Mr. Wada had to bend over and hold his stomach from laughing too hard.

Emi thought that Rev. Kichisaburo Okura was probably the most interesting visitor Mama and Papa ever had from Japan. In fact, she liked him quite a lot.

Promptly at 8:30, Mr. Wada's head began to nod.

"Ojii-chan is getting sleepy," Mrs. Wada said. "It is past his bedtime."

Benji, too, was beginning to bat his eyelids, like the wings of a tired butterfly.

"Didn't I tell you he might be nice?" Mrs. Wada whispered to Emi as she put on her coat.

Emi nodded. Mrs. Wada was right.

"So your birthday wasn't spoiled after all."

Emi shook her head. It had turned out, in fact, to be one of the nicest birthdays she'd ever had.

Benji had to tell Emi what he liked best about her birthday before he went home. "I liked the ice cream and cake best," he said. Then, just as he was going out the door, he added, "But the funeral was good too."

"It sure was," Emi agreed. "It was all good. Everything."

"I'm glad," Mama said, putting her arm around Emi's shoulders. "I'm glad your birthday turned out to be so nice."

Papa saw that Benji got safely inside his house, and then he put Mr. and Mrs. Wada in his car. "I'll be back soon," he called, and drove off into the night.

Emi never liked having people leave her birthday parties. It was as though her birthday were vanishing a little bit with each of them. Tonight, when they closed the door, she was glad that Rev. Okura was still there sitting on the sofa. He had slipped off his shoes again and was wriggling his toes.

"What a nice celebration on my first day in America," he said, looking contented. Even his feet looked happy.

"I'm so glad you'll be staying with us for a while," Mama said.

"Me too," Emi said, and she truly meant it.

Then she plopped down on the sofa beside Rev. Okura, kicked off her own shoes, and let the full joy of her birthday reach all the way down to her toes.